P9-DND-803

FAIRY TALE
FRANKIE

✳ and the ✳

Tricky Witch

For Anne—G. G.

For my wonderful teacher Mrs. Wood,
who inspired so many—S. L.

ALADDIN

An imprint of Simon & Schuster Children's Publishing Division
1230 Avenue of the Americas, New York, New York 10020
First Aladdin hardcover edition October 2016
Text copyright © 2016 by Greg Gormley
Illustrations copyright © 2016 by Steven Lenton
Originally published in Great Britain by Hachette Children's Books UK.
All rights reserved, including the right of reproduction in whole or in part in any form.
ALADDIN is a trademark of Simon & Schuster, Inc., and related logo
is a registered trademark of Simon & Schuster, Inc.
For information about special discounts for bulk purchases, please contact
Simon & Schuster Special Sales at 1-866-506-1949 or business@simonandschuster.com.
The Simon & Schuster Speakers Bureau can bring authors to your live event.
For more information or to book an event contact the
Simon & Schuster Speakers Bureau at 1-866-248-3049 or
visit our website at www.simonspeakers.com.
Book designed by Karina Granda
The text of this book was set in Olympian LT STD.
Manufactured in China 0716 SUK
1 2 3 4 5 6 7 8 9 10
Library of Congress Control Number 2015952122
ISBN 978-1-4814-6625-7 (hc)
ISBN 978-1-4814-6626-4 (eBook)

FAIRY TALE FRANKIE

and the

Tricky Witch

By Greg Gormley

Illustrated by Steven Lenton

ALADDIN NEW YORK LONDON TORONTO SYDNEY NEW DELHI

Frankie loved fairy tales.

She really, **really** loved them.

So one morning, she was rather surprised and delighted to find . . .

. . . a fairy tale **princess** in her bedroom!

"Please, could you help me hide?"
said the princess. "The WITCH
is COMING!"

"Yes, of course!" said Frankie.
"You can hide under my bed."

Then Frankie opened her bedroom door, only to find a unicorn's bottom blocking her path.

"I don't know where to hide," said the unicorn, panicking, "AND THE WITCH IS ON HER WAY!"

This was all quite unusual, but Frankie adored unicorns, so she pushed it into her wardrobe.

"Please, could you pass me my overalls?" she asked, before carefully closing the door.

Frankie got dressed and went to the bathroom, where she noticed a **mermaid** peeping out from the bathtub.

"WOW! Hello!" said Frankie.

"Shhhhhhh," whispered the mermaid.

"I'm hiding from the witch. Would you help me?"

"Of course!" said Frankie as she drew the shower curtain. "That should do the trick."

Frankie zipped downstairs.

"If the witch **IS** coming, I should
find my sneakers, just in case
I need to run," said Frankie.

She heard a
clinking
sound and saw
two boots
sticking out from
under the coats. . . .

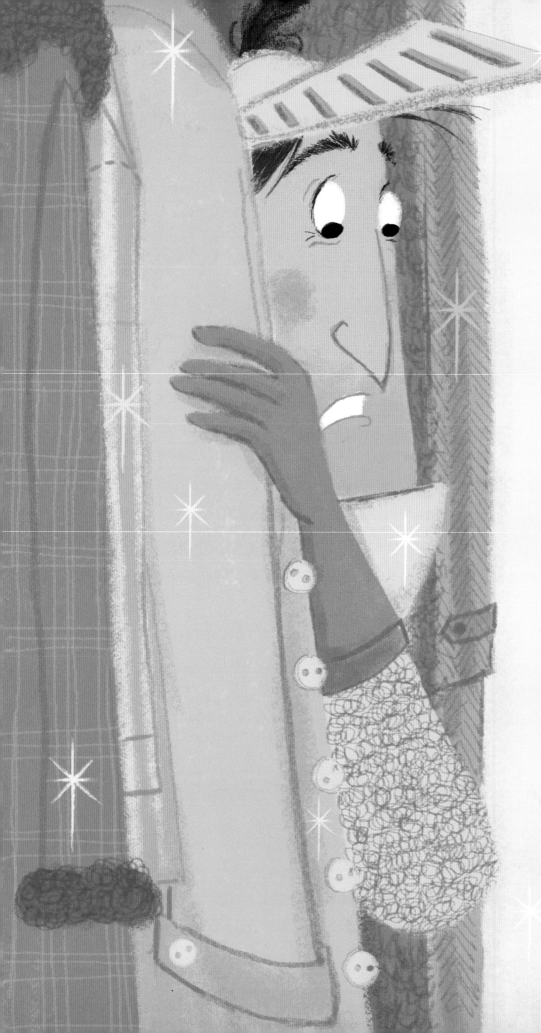

"Who's there?" said Frankie.

"A brave knight," said the knight, shaking. **"I'M TRYING TO HIDE FROM THE WITCH!"**

"Well, that doesn't seem very brave," said Frankie.

"You'd better come and have some breakfast."
Frankie gave the knight a piece of toast, then hid
him among the pots and pans under the sink.

As Frankie poured her cereal, a small frog hopped out of the box—*crunch!*

"What are you doing in my breakfast?" said Frankie.

"Hiding," said the frog.

"Well, jump back in the box," said Frankie.

"Can I have a kiss?" asked the frog.

"Certainly not," said Frankie as the doorbell rang.

There was a **king** at the door.

"Don't tell me," said Frankie.
"You need to hide from the witch."

"Correct," said the king. "Somewhere
fit for royalty, please!"

"Quick, under here," said Frankie. She placed a lampshade on the king's head and made him stand in the hallway.

"Oh . . . ," said the king.

Frankie looked around.

She had hidden everyone.

"But who will hide me?" said Frankie.

It was too late. . . .

KAZHAM!

The door crashed open and the witch appeared in a puff of smoke. **"Got you!"** the witch shrieked. "Now, where are the others?"

Frankie wanted to run.

It took every bit of her courage to say, "I don't know who you could possibly mean."

"Then there's only one thing to do!" said the witch, waving her pointy fingers in the air. **"Broom, Broom, bring them to me!"**

With a **WHOOSH**, the witch's broomstick sped through the house. It swept the princess from under the bed. "Careful!" she said.

It shoved the unicorn out of the wardrobe. "How rude!" he said.

It brushed the mermaid out of the bath. "That tickles!" she laughed.

The broom waggled around under the sink until out clattered the knight—*clank!*

It tipped over the cereal, and out tumbled the frog—

crackle!

Finally, it knocked the lampshade off the king's head—

clonk!

"Stop!" said Frankie.

"Leave my friends alone."

But the witch just cackled, "I've found you ALL. . . .

Whose turn is it now?"

"Turn? What do you mean?"
asked Frankie, puzzled.

"We're playing hide-and-seek,"
said the king. "Would you
like to play too?"

"Oh, yes please!" said Frankie.
"I love hide-and-seek!"

"Excellent," said the witch. "Now shut your eyes and count to ten while we hide."

Frankie shut her eyes and counted to ten, and then she called . . .

"Ready or not, here I come!"